WHO MADE YOU THE BOSS?

This is a Rapscallion Press production, brought to the page by the Rapscallion content team – Virginia McLean, Felicia Jackson and Rhian Sellier.

Illustrations by Nathan Hill.

Visit us at www.rapscallionpress.com

Printed by Wai Man Book Binding (China) Ltd.

Print production systems registered to ISO 14001: ISO 9001 Occupational Health and Safety Management System OHSAS 18001 Social Accountability Standard SA 8000

First published in Great Britain 2017 by Rapscallion Press Limited, 39A Princess Road, London, NW18JS. Company No. 09461707

Text and illustrations copyright © 2017 Rapscallion Press Ltd Designed by Jeni Child

ISBN 978-1-911017-04-2

CIP catalogue record for this title is available from The British Library.

WHO MADE YOU THE BOSS?

BY **THE RAPSCALLIONS**

ILLUSTRATED BY **NATHAN HILL**

CHAPTER 1

ANOTHER BRICK IN THE WALL

Toby pulled the duvet over his head. He thought about his Tuesday timetable: Double Maths, Double English, Tiny Break, Double Geography, Double Trouble, Slightly Less Tiny Break… Ugh.

He couldn't see how sitting in stuffy classrooms, or any of it, was going to help him in life. He wanted a job, in the real world.

At his school there was always someone bigger, smarter, stronger, more handsome, better at talking to girls than Toby was. Not that he wanted to be good at talking to girls, he just knew it was a thing.

The thought of toast and tea got him up and dressed.

"I really don't want to go to school today," he said wearily, as he reached the bottom of the stairs, to no-one in particular and not for the first time.

"You know Mum and Dad will go to prison if we don't

go to school." His big sister Lil always had an answer to everything. Sometimes she had an answer when there hadn't even been a question.

"You should read the article I just finished for the school paper. Our Big Debate of the week was: Does Education Prepare us for the Real World?"

Toby never read Lil's articles.

Another Brick in the Wall

"We might not go to prison just yet," winked Dad, on his way out the door, "but it is the law in this country that children have to be in full-time education."

"Who makes these laws?" muttered Toby, to no-one in particular, and not for the first time.

Buttered toast in mouth and shrugging on his coat Toby paused to scrutinise a framed fuzzy black-and-white photograph on the wall in the hallway.

Two big front teeth dominating a cheeky grin under an incomprehensibly messy mop of curly hair stared back at Toby. It was his Great Uncle Alfie as a child on his parent's farm in South America. He hadn't gone to school. Great Uncle Alfie had gone to the School of Life. And he'd ended up OK hadn't he? Well apart from that small matter of the purple parrot caper…

CHAPTER 2

THE FUTURE'S ORANGE

"...And so today, as a very special surprise treat..." Toby had dozed off during Miss Lemonsqueezy's third morning assembly that week on the perils of Fake News but the word 'treat' brought his attention back to the room.

"...please welcome Kodomo Kyasaki from the wonderful technology company Manners Incorporated, who is here with some exciting news!"

The Hall fell into a stunned silence for a split second – as if suspended in time – and then erupted in a cacophony of cheers, claps, whoops, whistles and the drumming of feet.

Manners, Inc. was the Coolest. Full Stop. Company. Full stop. Known to any child. Full. Dot. Stop.

A serene huge-eyed young woman wearing a distinct red kimono, covered in little 'M's', took to the stage.

Chapter 2

"Children of Comfort Falls Primary," began Kodomo Kyasaki in a sweet, soothing voice, "Mike Manners has asked me to come in person here today, to ask you to be the very first children in this country to try out his brand new Oggle Goggles."

Every new gadget Manners, Inc. produced was hotly anticipated.

It was several minutes before order could be restored by Miss Lemonsqueezy.

"There is a very special prize draw - the winner will have the chance to work at Manners, Inc. Please come up and collect your pair of Goggles for the day," finished Kodomo with a mysterious smile.

The thought crossed Toby's mind that his Tuesday was actually turning out a lot better than he'd anticipated. He had to win that prize. He wanted that job. He did not want to waste another minute at school. "I should be able to work in the real world if I want to," he mumbled, to no-one in particular, and not for the first time.

Miss Lemonsqueezy led the whole school out of assembly, the children clutching their Goggles.

Lil waited behind, recording device in hand, to interview Kodomo for that week's paper. "Miss Kyasaki, tell me, why are you visiting schools at this time?"

The Future's Orange

"At Manners, Inc. we have created technology that can completely immerse people in a perfect world. We are looking for the best minds to help us create that world and we've found that children have the clearest, brightest, most un-spoilt vision – so where better to test our products than in schools?"

"And what would you say to those who claim that Oggle Goggles are just another device that distract children from using their imaginations?"

"You have courage, for a young reporter," Kodomo's eyes fixed laser-like on Lil's, "But your questions will have to wait. You'd better join your friends now and get to class." And with that, Kodomo ushered Lil back down the corridor.

Chapter 2

✿ ✿ ✿ ✿

Toby meanwhile, had ducked behind the heavy fire doors to the assembly hall as the rest of the children and teachers migrated back to their classrooms in an undulating swarm of chatter and excitement. He wanted to try on his super high tech high definition hyper-real new-wide-world creators in peace and quiet.

Hands trembling, he held the Goggles up to his eyes. What he saw made him draw a breath in amazement – it felt like he was seeing a perfect world for the first time. A world where happy children were driving around in shiny new cars, working in little pods coming up with ideas for computer games. It was his fantasy, the place he went when he daydreamed about not having to go to school, but even better.

".....at Manners, Inc. children lead productive, well rewarded and fulfilled working lives," a beguiling voice began. "They avoid eleven years of tedium in a school system designed to take the power, the fun, and the rewards away from them. Working for Manners, Inc. children get to use their vivid and highly imaginative minds to create the technological content of the future. In return they are given, not only independence from the drudgery of school, but also daily rewards and compensation for their efforts. Come and see for yourselves at Manners, Inc., Manners Tower, Mannerstown, Manners Island.

[In a very fast voice like on the credit card advertisements] "Applicants must be 3 years or over, sartorially and hygienically independent. Manners, Inc. is a self-regulating body and accepts no liability for injuries or harm incurred."

A hand suddenly clasped his shoulder. Toby jumped out of his skin, the Oggle Goggles tumbling to the floor. As he scrambled to retrieve them he looked up into the huge, soulful eyes of Kodomo Kyasaki.

"Miss Kyasaki! Er, this is incredible! These Oggle Goggles are even higher definition than the Pineapple Phone GX! This sort of tech wasn't supposed to be available for another 30 years!" Toby exclaimed breathlessly.

"I see you're already a convert," she smiled, "I have a feeling you might be just the sort of person Mike Manners needs at Manners, Inc. right now. What's your name?"

"T..T..Toby," he stammered.

Chapter 2

"I think I've found my prize draw winner," she said.

"Really? But you haven't picked the actual winner yet, have you? I mean don't get me wrong, I'm OK with it and everything but I think a lot of the other kids are going to be a bit annoy..."

"Sometimes Toby," Kodomo interrupted, "Winners make their own luck."

Toby reckoned his Great Uncle Alfie would have agreed with that statement.

He followed Kodomo out of school in a daze of excitement.

CHAPTER 3

WHO LET THE DOGS OUT?

Back in her classroom, Lil watched the advert from Manners, Inc. through her Oggle Goggles and thought, "That is sooooo fake and cheesy. I'm just waiting for the pink fluffy unicorns to appear".

Something about that so-called perfect world and that Kodomo was not ringing true for Lil. There was a story there somewhere and she would find it.

Removing the Oggles, some movement out in the car park caught her eye through the large, Victorian classroom window.

"Toby?! What's he doing going off with Kodomo?!"

At that very moment, the bell rang for Tiny Break and Lil pelted out to the playground, just in time to see Toby disappearing into the front seat of a sleek black Model ZED SUV.

Chapter 3

Lil ducked and scurried as fast as she could, hunched over and unseen by Toby and the driver. She silently slipped into the back seat of the car.

She pulled the door shut quietly and crouched trembling in the foot-well behind the elegant figure of Kodomo Kyasaki in the driver's seat. The thought occurred to Lil that this was either the smartest – or dumbest – thing she'd ever done. Either way, she chose to remain hidden and get as close to the truth as possible.

As they moved smoothly off, Toby noticed Kodomo's hands were nowhere near the wheel.

"This is driverless?!" he exclaimed.

This day just could not get any better.

"We're making one stop before Manners, Inc. Toby," said Kodomo in her silky smooth voice. "We're off to the Prime Minister's office at No 10, Eiderdown Street. I've got some very important documents from Mr Manners that I need Prime Minister Digby Davenport to sign, won't take long."

❁ ❁ ❁ ❁

Sometime later Lil had the worst pins and needles in her left foot. She peeked out of the window just as the shiny black car drove straight past number 10, Eiderdown St, and turned right up a gloomy, cobbled alleyway, pulling up next to a large blue wooden door and some green wheelie bins.

Kodomo grabbed her briefcase and leapt nimbly out of the car. "I'll be quick as a flash, Toby. Wait here and for goodness' sake, please don't touch anything!" She knocked three times on the blue door using a huge brass knocker in the shape of a lion's head. The door opened a crack and she slipped inside the building.

Toby looked around enthusiastically at all the tempting technology and shiny buttons and levers in the futuristic car.

"Pssst!"

He jumped out of his skin for the second time that day.

"What the...!"

Lil had crawled out from the back of the car into the alley by the bins, and was gesturing wildly through the windscreen for Toby to get out.

"Lil???" exclaimed Toby, lowering the window and sticking his head out.

"Toby, we've got to get away from here, you're crazy going off with her. We don't know the first thing about her and..."

"But Lil, I won the prize draw. I'm on my way to start my job at Manners, Inc., what's the problem? You're the crazy one, hiding in there all this time!!!"

"Toby, if you don't get out of this car right now I'm calling Dad."

Toby grudgingly got out of the car into the shadowy passage, and came over to Lil.

"Okay Okay, just stop shouting. Kodomo will be back any second and I'm not going anywhere…"

He was cut off by a sharp pain in his right ankle. He grabbed it, hopping on his left leg and screaming 'Ow, Ow, Ow, what did you do that fo…"

Who Let the Dogs Out?

"Yap yap! Yap yap yap! Yap yap yap yap!"

Toby hopped and stumbled backwards into a wheelie bin.

Three tiny vicious animals were staring up at him with pointy ears and stubby tails aloft, front paws planted firmly, and baring their razor-sharp teeth in menacing grimaces.

Just then a shiny blond head appeared, a gloved hand stretched out, and a voice said, "Oh good afternoon. I'm Penelope, Sir Digby Davenport's daughter. How delightful to meet you," as if, for all the world, she were meeting them at a garden party at Buckingham Palace, rather than by the bins, in an alley behind the kitchen.

Toby looked up from his wheelie bin slightly dazed, covered in tea bags and banana peel and besieged by the monsters, which he now recognised as some variety of miniature dog.

"I'm Toby," he managed, over the yapping.

"And I'm Lil, his sister."

Penelope looked at them quizzically. "Might I be able to assist you with anything?"

"I'm trying to persuade my lunk-head brother that he can't just give up school, go off with this Kodomo

Chapter 3

person, and get a job at Manners, Inc." said Lil glaring at Toby almost as menacingly as Penelope's mini guard dogs, who had stopped yapping and simmered down to a low growl.

"Do you know, Lil – oh that's funny, my great Auntie's called Lil, well, Elizabeth, to be precise. We call her Great Auntie Lil. Anyway, I digress… yes as I was saying, I agree with you one hundred percent. There is something distinctly fishy about Mr Manners. He comes and visits Daddy in a loud and garish gold jet. And as for his son Mike Jr.! I sat next to him recently at a State banquet – although the rumour is he's a scientific genius, he spent the entire meal on his Pineapple Phone GX. Most impolite.

"Footsie! Dow! Jones! Do be good dogs and leave these poor children alone," commanded Penelope.

"Come inside for some tea and crumpets," she trilled, "I do some of my best persuading on a full tummy".

CHAPTER 4

YOU ONLY SING WHEN YOU'RE WINNING

They sat in silence until Penelope had finished her crumpet, patted her mouth delicately with a napkin and asked, "Now Toby, what's this I hear about you not wanting to go to school?"

Toby told her excitedly about how Kodomo had visited their school, how amazing Manners, Inc. was and how he'd won the chance to have an internship and that he wanted to work and develop fantastic computer games and make money instead of going to school.

"But Toby, compulsory education for children has been the law here since the 1880 Education Act," explained Penelope, "that can't be changed just for you."

"Well here's a heads up: IT'S NOT 1880 ANYMORE!" sputtered Toby, mouth full of crumpet. "And who exactly makes these stupid laws, anyway?"

You Only Sing When You're Winning

"Toby! Don't be so rude," said Lil.

"In this country we have had a proud tradition of representative democracy since the Glorious Revolution of 1688," lectured Penelope. "Powers of sovereignty are delegated to a body of men, elected from time to time, who exercise these powers for the benefit of the whole nation…"

All Toby could hear was "Blah, blah, blah blah blah". This was worse than school. He yawned theatrically.

"Imagine it's like… football," appealed Penelope, in a desperate attempt to get through to him.

"Football – what on earth has it got to do with football?" asked Toby sceptically.

"Yes, what does it have to do with football?" echoed Lil, quietly switching on her recording device just in case.

"Everyone over the age of 18 gets to vote for a player from their neighbourhood. BUT, you not only need to like the player, also the team he or she is playing for.

"Let's say there's a yellow team, a green team and an orange team.

"I know I don't like the yellow team, I quite like the green and orange teams but prefer the player on the green team, let's call him Bob. So I vote for Bob on the green team. Turns out Bob is pretty popular in my area and gets more votes than the other two. Bob then plays for my neighbourhood on the green team."

Toby sat down again, able to imagine the teams and the players in his head.

"Now here's the difference between an election and football match. It's not the number of goals you score that means you win or lose, but the number of players you manage to get on your team. The biggest team wins.

You Only Sing When You're Winning

"All the most popular football players (in real life they are called MPs) from each neighbourhood get to play, but because one team is bigger, it's more powerful. Even though we voted for Bob and the green team, the orange team has ended up with more players, so they win.

"Each team has a captain, and the captain of the biggest team becomes the boss or the Prime Minister."

"Like your Dad, Sir Digby Davenport," added Lil, "who's boss of the orange team."

"Indeed," agreed Penelope.

"I get it," said Toby, who really was grateful that Penelope had worked out a way to explain it to him. "So it's about being popular?" he was fascinated. "Like a singing contest? Sing the loudest and the best and hey presto! Victory is yours?"

"When you put it like that, it does sound a bit mad!" Lil agreed.

"Well, the biggest problem I have with all of this," declared Toby, "is that we don't even get to vote, and we're the ones that have to do what these people say."

"Well it's actually worse than that," admitted Penelope. "Although everyone aged 18 and over (not in prison) is allowed to vote (that's about 70% of the population), only about half of them ever actually do."

Chapter 4

"What?" shouted Toby angrily, jumping to his feet again. "So all these laws and rules that I have to follow are being made by a bunch of people that not even half the country voted for?

"That's ridiculous. It's not fair. There has to be a better way. I want to give the School of Life a go, like Great Uncle Alfie did, Lil". His sister looked puzzled. "Tell Dad not to worry, I'll be in touch soon." Toby called over his shoulder, as he bolted out of the Davenport's kitchen.

"Toby!" cried Lil.

CHAPTER 5

GOING UNDERGROUND

Lil turned aghast to Penelope, "Help me stop him. If he finds Kodomo he'll go off with her to Manners, Inc. and we might never see him again!" she pleaded.

"That's Footsie, Dow and Jones barking!" exclaimed Penelope. "They must have found Toby."

The girls scurried down what appeared to be an endless succession of carpeted corridors with sombre portraits of serious looking people, mostly men. Lil noticed only two female faces. The Chihuahuas could be heard barking behind a door. Penelope burst through.

A rather plummy voice said disapprovingly, "Poppy darling, Daddy is very busy running the country, and..."

"Oh Daddy! Stop being so silly! I am sure the country can run perfectly well without you for a few minutes."

Sir Digby, was sitting pompously at his desk. Opposite

him was Kodomo, with a firm grip on Toby, and surrounded by the three yapping Chihuahuas.

"Let go of my brother, now!" cried Lil, lunging towards Toby.

"What do you think you're doing?!" roared Sir Digby, who wasn't used to that sort of behaviour in his office.

A split second of surprise was all it took for Kodomo to lose her grip on Toby.

In a flash, Penelope grabbed a bewildered Toby by his hoodie and Lil by the hand, and pulled them both into a nearby cupboard. Just as Toby and Lil were beginning to panic at the small cramped space, Penelope held her watch up to a sensor in the back wall and the whole panel slid open, revealing a bare concrete and glass corridor beyond.

As the girls started to run, dragging a reluctant Toby between them, Penelope's watch buzzed, lighting up with an orange alert.

She glanced down at it and then stopped in her tracks. "This could be serious. Dramatic change of plan I'm afraid. You two need to come with me. I could do with some extra bodies on this. We'll address Toby's authority issues later.

"We'll use the SSSS," said Penelope. Toby and Lil looked at her, both equally mystified.

"Of course, I'm so sorry. I haven't had a chance to explain. The Super-Secret-Subway-System (SSSS for short) connects all the countries in the world, in an intricate network of supersonic connections," explained Penelope. "It is used by the CWLC – The Children of World Leaders' Club – in our mission to keep our parents from messing up.

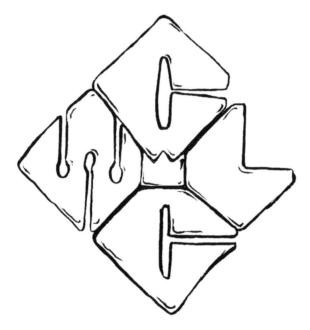

"To use it you need to wear this special wristband," she handed Toby and Lil each a band bearing a CWLC logo.

Penelope tapped the SSSS icon on her smart-watch, and a very calm, mannerly voice asked, "Where are you headed today, Miss Penelope?"

Going Underground

"To visit Chen," Penelope replied.

"A subway heading that way should be with you in... three seconds," replied the voice.

The children felt an immensely powerful whoosh of warm wind and a subway carriage appeared right beside them, its doors gliding gently open.

Penelope ushered them in – "DO mind the gap and take a seat quickly," and the doors slid shut, bam! behind them.

Chapter 5

Toby and Lil sat obediently, blinking in the brightly lit carriage. They gripped their armrests tightly as the train jolted off and flung them this way and that along dark tunnels at lightning speed, with a deafening roar. Toby was just opening his mouth to holler at Penelope when the roar subsided and they slowed down. His mouth remained agape as he gazed out at the most incredible sight: what looked like a giant prawn with orange whiskers was sailing past the carriage window.

"What's going on?" asked Lil, "Why have we slowed down? Where are we?".

"We just have to make sure we don't scare the sea cucumbers, snail fish and supergiant crustaceans that live in the Mariana trench," replied Penelope who prided herself in being a friend to all  creatures and who was personally behind this 'go-slow' initiative. "We are almost 7 miles down now," she informed them, "the deepest part of the ocean, which means we're nearly at our destination."

A moment later, the train jerked to a halt, the doors of the carriage flew open and Penelope urged them to get out quickly.

CHAPTER 6

ALL FOR ONE

Before they could protest, Toby and Lil followed Penelope straight into a cupboard just like the one in Sir Digby's office. Penelope held up her watch and another door slid open.

They emerged into an enormous grey concrete square, one side of which was lined with red flags on poles. A giant picture of an elderly man with very plump cheeks grinned down at them.

Rushing towards them was a trendily dressed boy, black hair gelled into a perfect quiff. "Penelope!"

"Toby, Lil, meet Chen," said Penelope, "Tech genius of the CWLC, when he is not working as a top international singer/actor/model."

"We'll need to leave the introductions for later Pen," said Chen. "We're holding a crisis briefing for all CWLC agents right now."

All for One

Toby and Lil looked at each other, wide-eyed. Lil took Toby's hand and for the first time since he was 4 years old, he didn't protest. They hurried after Chen and Penelope.

They arrived in a briefing room with a giant wall of TV screens linked to the CWLC agents in the 196 countries of the world.

"Now you're here Pen, we can start." Chen called up images on a central holographic display of over a 1000 school classrooms. "These are from all around our country. Note that in each one there are empty rows where children are missing."

"Looks almost as boring as my classroom. No wonder kids are skipping school," grumbled Toby. He snuck a glance around the room for an easy exit, keen to find Kodomo as soon as he could.

Chapter 6

Chen turned to Toby angrily and said, "You don't understand, school in my country is a serious business. Unlike your paltry 7 hours, we go to school for 10 hours a day, and then get 2–4 hours homework every night, and 14 hours at weekends.

"Teachers demand and get respect, and because of the old one child policy, pressure to do well from family is intense. The attention, expectations and family honour of parents and grandparents is all on you.

"Children here do not just 'skip' school," said Chen firmly.

"Who the heck would make rules like that?!" scoffed Toby.

Chen turned to face Toby. "You have absolutely no idea about life in the rest of the world, do you? You're really beginning to get on my nerves.

"You want to know who makes the laws in this country? Well, since the Revolution in 1949, one party – The Party – rules and makes all the laws.

"Before the Revolution what percentage of people could read or write? Only 20%. That's right a measly 1 in 5," said Chen, on a roll. "What's the percentage now? Close to 100%. To what age were people expected to live to before the revolution? 35. What age do people live to now? 75. The changes The Party made have improved the lives of all our people."

"OK, OK, I get it!" said Toby, chastened. "But what I don't get is how come there is only one 'team' playing in the competition to run the country? How can you play a game with only one team?"

"We don't play a game or have a competition to decide how to run our country, that would be a crazy idea!" exclaimed Chen impatiently. "My father President Ping, together with a wise committee, leads The Party fairly and with only good intentions and the best interests of all citizens at heart."

"Now boys and girls, we have more important things to do than argue over political systems," interjected Penelope. "We still have to find out why these pupils are missing and where they might have gone."

Lil was scrutinising one of the holographic images. "There, what's that on the wall in the corner of the class-room in zone three?" she pointed. "It's a Manners, Inc. poster, like the ones we had up in our school, before Kodomo's visit."

Chapter 6

"Great spot Lil," said Chen, making her blush. "Zoom out on those other classrooms, let's see if we can see that Manners, Inc. poster anywhere else?"

"Why, it's in all of them!" cried Penelope.

There was no question about it. Someone from Manners, Inc. had visited all these classrooms with Oggle Goggles and children had disappeared.

"We need to find out where Kodomo is going next, before more school children disappear."

Toby noticed the tiniest flash of Kodomo's red kimono with the little 'M's' on it disappearing off the bottom left hand of a CWLC monitor.

Toby pointed at the screen and asked Chen, "Where's that?" Chen glanced up at the screen, "That's the home of Anaya, our ninja specialist, based in the Kingdom of Phat. Why do you ask?"

"I was just wanting to find out more about life in the rest of the world – you know expand my horizons, like you said," replied Toby cheekily.

Chen rolled his eyes and turned back to Penelope and Lil, who were busy poring over a 3D holographic map of the globe.

Toby backed silently out of the briefing room, and

once out of the door, sped towards the cupboard where they'd exited the SSSS. Heart pounding, he got in to the waiting carriage and – just as Penelope had done – tapped the SSSS icon on his CWLC wristband, instructing the train to take him to the Kingdom of Phat.

CHAPTER 7

BORN TO
BE WILD

The sides of the carriage rattled as the train roared along and Toby's face tightened from the pressure. This Tuesday was not short of thrills, he had to admit that. Lil would just have to understand: winners make their own luck.

He was back on track, so to speak, now that he'd managed to ditch that bossy Penelope and that international model/singer/geek/whatever Chen…

But before he could finish the thought, the train came to an abrupt stop and Toby stumbled forwards through the open doors and into a small, now familiar-looking cupboard.

Enclosed in the tiny space, he tried swiping his bracelet on the back wall as he'd seen Pen do, but something was wrong. His breath came quickly and there was a tightening sensation in his chest – he could feel a hot panic flushing his cheeks.

He started to bang on the door, worried about drawing attention to himself but seeing no alternative.

The door slid open and Toby gasped with relief at the sight of a short, slender, athletic-looking girl, standing in a lush tropical courtyard.

"Anaya?" breathed Toby tentatively.

"Yes," she replied enquiringly, "how do you know my name? Are you CWLC?" she asked, glancing down at his wristband.

"Yes, I'm Toby and I'm working with Penelope Davenport. She sent me to you to check out a report we received that your schools were being visited by Kodomo of Manners, Inc." Just a little teensy weensy alternative fact-slash-white lie never hurt anyone, thought Toby smiling to himself.

"If she is visiting," replied Anaya, "I'm afraid I'm not aware of it, as some people here don't even think girls need a full and proper education.

"Although this will change if I get my way." she said determinedly. "I'm already the equivalent of a black belt in Jeet Kun Do, Ninjutsu, and Bokator. You might have seen me competing under the name Lethal Leopard in the World Wrestling Slap Up?"

Toby allowed himself to be impressed and just a little bit scared.

"But, that aside," Anaya said, "I'm happy to help if Penelope thinks it's a good idea. Let's go ask my Dad – he knows Mike Manners personally. I think they do Book Club together…"

Two guards carrying ornamental ostrich feathered spears appeared on either side of Anaya.

"Your father requests your presence in the throne room, Princess Anaya. He would like to know why you are conversing unaccompanied with this young gentleman."

Toby gulped.

Anaya winked at him as they followed the implacable guards into a magnificent palace and down silk-carpeted hallways. "Don't be frightened," she whispered, "Dad thinks he's in charge of everything but he doesn't usually imprison my friends, at least not unless I recommend it…"

Sitting on a heavily carved golden throne was King Phat himself, sporting aviator sunglasses and dressed in a highly ornate, green and gold soldier's uniform, embellished with medals, gemstones and sparkling epaulettes.

"Dad, were you expecting a visit from anyone from Manners, Inc. today?" asked Anaya.

Born to be Wild

"Who, my little pumpkin?"

"You know, the makers of those amazing Oggle Goggles."

"Not those dreadful things... I've spent twenty years educating and providing for my loving people so that they can look after themselves and feed and clothe their families. They do not need to live in Mr Mike Manners' imaginary worlds: we have all we need to be happy right here in the fabulous Kingdom of Phat. I'm thinking of having those Goggley thingies banned," announced King Phat.

"Wow, can you do that?" asked Toby incredulously.

"I can do whatever I wish," announced King Phat. "I am the supreme ruler, as was my father, and his father, and his father before him. The Phat family were victorious in the great battle of long ago and have ruled the Kingdom ever since."

"Sounds reasonable." Toby remembered how angry Chen had become when he questioned the way they did things in his country. He certainly didn't have time to risk the wrath of the Phat family if he was going to find his way to Manners, Inc. (though he knew Lil would definitely have had something to say about girls not having the choice to go school).

He changed the subject. "But Your Royal Phatness, I am sure a lady called Kodomo was here. I saw the sleeve of her kimono in a picture being transmitted from right here in the Kingdom of Phat. It's very distinctive – red with little M's on it."

"Oh, you mean Miss Kyasaki, who works for Mike?" asked King Phat. "She was here, reporting in, ahem, I mean coming to pay tribute," he coughed. "She gave me a lovely pair of the latest M-shades which will go nicely with my new outfit."

"Where is she now sir? I have to find her," said Toby urgently.

"She's gone, but she left a business card with directions to her office," said King Phat, and Toby reached out for it and bowed as low as he could, thinking that that was probably what you did with Supreme Rulers.

CHAPTER 8

MISSION POSSIBLE?

Back in the crisis briefing room, members of the Children of the World Leaders Club all over the globe were reporting thousands of children missing from classrooms. All had Manners, Inc. posters on their walls.

"We need to get as much information as possible on Mike Manners and his organisation," suggested Lil, now in full Clark Kent/investigative journalist mode. "We need to scan every available article, tweet, blog and post from Manners, Inc. and anyone connected to them."

"OK, from what we have gathered from the media coverage so far, on the surface, Mike Manners appears to be just another billionaire – a gifted businessman and owner of a vast technology and real estate empire," said Chen.

"But according to this latest intelligence coming in from CWLC agents," continued Penelope, "his plan seems to be to recruit hundreds of thousands of children just like Toby by telling them they don't need to go to school, but can earn money and independence by working for him instead."

"He keeps his son, Manners Junior or MJ, closely under his control," Chen added. "And there are rumours that MJ has developed some kind of cutting edge technology to use children's imaginations to create the never–before–seen virtual reality scenarios in Manners World. And wait, this sounds crazy but it says here that they are knocked out, put in pods and hooked up to electrodes!"

Chen's brow furrowed as he continued to read.

"Apparently, people have become so addicted to these virtual 'perfect' Manners' Worlds that they are signing up to them full-time, leaving the real world behind, and allowing Manners full control of their virtual lives. Some parents are even putting Oggles on new-borns so that they will grow up never having seen the real world."

"We must assemble an advance crack team and infiltrate Manners, Inc. now!" declared Penelope. "Myself to lead, Chen on tech and call Anaya from the Kingdom of Phat to be the muscle. Lil and Toby, stay put - you'll be safe here."

"This is awful. Can you see now Toby why we can't let you go and work for Manners, Inc.?

"Toby? ...Are you listening to me, Toby?" Lil swung around scanning the room for her brother.

Mission Possible?

"No, no, no, I can't find Toby!" Lil cried out. "Pen, Chen - help me, I think he's gone!"

Chen remembered, "Toby was asking about one of the screens, the one from the Kingdom of Phat. I didn't know why he was interested at the time."

"I'll check the log for the journeys made on Toby's CWLC band," said Penelope, "Yes, here it is, he took a train to the Kingdom of Phat just 10 minutes ago. Hang on. He seems to be boarding another train. Where's it going?... Oh no! It's heading straight to Manners, Inc."

"How could he have done that? I should have been looking after him. How will we get him back? My Dad's going to kill me," blurted Lil.

"Chen, is there any chance you can stop him by disabling the SSSS function on his wristband?" asked Penelope.

"I'll try," said Chen, tapping fiercely at his keyboard.

"Lost him," said Chen, "he's out of our jurisdiction. He's now in an information-censored area controlled by Manners, Inc."

"Let's get this crack team together and get going!" encouraged Lil, feeling a surge of determination to get her brother back.

"We'll make a plan on the way...and don't worry, I'll bring the crumpets." said Penelope.

CHAPTER 9

ROCK-A-BYE

Toby's train had arrived at Manners, Inc. station.

This time, rather than being empty, the arrival cupboard contained a shelf with glass of orange liquid on it. Next to it was a sign saying, "Drink Me."

"Now where have I seen that before…" he muttered to himself, not keen to try it. He looked around him for a way out, frantically swiping his wristband over each of the cupboard walls in turn.

"Drink the juice, Toby!" A stern voice over a loudspeaker startled him. "You will not gain entry to Manners, Inc. if you do not drink the drink."

Toby reached for the glass and with a trembling hand, brought it to his lips. "Smells OK. Here goes nothing!" And he downed it in one.

The wall next to him fell away to reveal what he could only describe as a 'perfect world': vivid bright colours around Toby sparkled in brilliant sunshine and smells of clean laundry mingled on the warm wind with sweet candy and freshly baked cinnamon rolls.

Kodomo greeted him, "Hi Toby, welcome to Manners, Inc. I am glad you finally made it." She seemed in a bit of a hurry, and was glancing around nervously, leading him into what looked like a large warehouse.

"I know you have been on a long tiring journey. Let me settle you down into your Manners-pod and you can relax. Just tick this box and you can go and get comfortable."

Toby read:
By ticking this box you agree to the terms and conditions below...

Toby ticked the box, yawning.

These were the kinds of Terms and Conditions he had seen on-line and had never bothered to read.

Feeling strangely tired, Toby had an overwhelming desire to shut his eyes. He allowed Kodomo to drop him into a luxury leather reclining seat, which nestled snug inside a white egg-shaped capsule.

"Shut your eyes, relax and think beautiful thoughts about your favourite things," said Kodomo, in her soft melodic voice. Toby's eyelids fluttered, "That liquid, what was in… that drink…" his faint voice trailed off and after a few shudders his breathing became slow and heavy. He was out for the count.

"Pod 56,981 is now dormant," reported Kodomo in a totally different, menacingly mechanical voice, "electrode helmet in place, ready to transmit." It was as if someone had flicked the switch on her mode button from 'caring manga girl' to 'heartless cyborg'.

"That's terrific Kodomo," said a slick-looking young guy with a punchy, New York accent. He ran a hand through his thick orange hair and pushed his tortoise-shell glasses up his nose. Looking up to a glass box suspended from the ceiling, he gave the thumbs up and said, "Latest brain download is finito Pops."

His father, Mike Manners, President of Manners, Inc. nodded proudly down at his son from his glass office and surveyed the tens of thousands of pods and the thousands of computer screens below him.

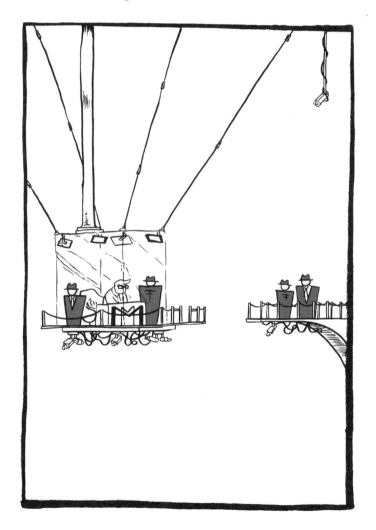

Rock-A-Bye

Each pod contained a working child whose vivid creative imagination was now feeding a virtual world; a Manners World, which was going to be viewed by the millions of people around the planet wearing his hyper-reality Oggle Goggles.

He pressed a button and his voice boomed out around the facility, "Bring me more children. I will use them very well. No one will use them better than me.

"We will make this planet pure again. We will make this planet safe again. We will make this planet strong again. We will make this planet great again."

Mike Junior cheered ecstatically, and joined in chanting, "Make this planet great again, make this planet great again."

CHAPTER 10

"HELLO FROM THE OTHER SIDE"

Anaya, a ninja hand-to-hand combat extraction specialist, had joined Pen, Chen and Lil on the SSSS train. She confirmed that she had met Toby, posing as a CWLC agent in the Kingdom of Phat, and that he'd been looking for Kodomo.

"Just wait till I get my hands on my brother," Lil was fuming. "How are we going to get him back?"

"My number one rule in these situations is: hope for the best and plan for the worst," said Penelope. "Ideas, anyone?"

"Let's introduce a bug into the computer system," said Chen.

"We could just break in and smash up his pod," suggested Anaya enthusiastically.

"Far too risky, I'm afraid. We are dealing with children's brains here, remember," said Penelope.

Suddenly there was a crackle coming from the loud-speaker and a holograph flickered to life in the centre of the carriage. They heard a faint voice and saw a wobbly blurred image of none other than Kodomo Kyasaki.

"Hello, is anyone there? I haven't got long, please acknowledge".

"Kodomo! Where's my brother? What have you done with him?" shouted Lil, lunging for the image.

"Hello, this is Penelope Davenport from the CWLC. What is the purpose of your call, Kyasaki San?"

"I am a covert operative at Manners, Inc. working for the WLC," replied Kodomo.

"The WLC? What's that?" whispered Lil.

"It's the Club all the parents of the CWLC belong to," whispered back Anaya, "Trust our parents to keep us out of the loop."

"I am transmitting on a secure WLC line, which may cut out any second so it can't be traced. I am in the Manners facility right now," continued Kodomo. "And I have Toby here."

"How do we know we can trust her? She's the one who kidnapped Toby and all those other children!" Lil cried desperately.

"Hello From the Other Side"

"I do also have thousands of other children," continued Kodomo. "Mike Manners sent me to lure them away from classrooms. I've had to play along so he would trust me, but I really am working for the WLC.

"You need to hurry. Many of the children have already been hooked up to Manners-pods. I have managed to keep them stable, so the process of draining their imaginations can be reversed, in theory anyway. It's never actually been tested."

"Kodomo, listen carefully," said Penelope. "We are on our way to you on the SSSS. I have Lil and two other elite members of the CWLC with me – Chen and Anaya. First we need to infiltrate the facility and secure Toby. What's his current status?"

"He is in a Manners-pod, wired up for imagination extraction," replied Kodomo. "Mike Junior thinks the procedure is complete, but I blocked the download from Toby and fed in an old one that was already in the system."

"Hello From the Other Side"

"Lovely work!" said Penelope.

"I've overridden the SSSS exit protocol so your CWLC wristband will open the cupboard directly inside the main gates.

"One problem though," added Kodomo. "I don't know how you will be able to get through Manners' Security system at the facility itself – it's triple-layered, motion sensitive and voice activated. And it's set up so only myself and Manners can gain entry."

Chen looked worried, "That security system is currently impenetrable."

"I don't know much about the other bits," Lil piped up, "but you mentioned it was voice-activated, and I do have a voice recording of Kodomo from when I was interviewing her for my article. Kodomo must be able to gain access, and I have her voice, so…"

"You might have cracked it Lil," said Chen, obviously impressed. "If I can use that recording I think Anaya and Pen can handle the rest."

"Now, assuming it works and we do get in, how many other pods are we looking at?" asked Penelope. "Any employees? Security? The location of Mike Manners? Mike Junior?"

Chapter 10

"There are 56,981 active pods, including Toby's," answered Kodomo's faint crackling voice, "Manners Junior built and operates the system on his own, and his father, Mike Manners, is in his office in a glass cube hanging from the ceiling, protected by 12 armed security guards.

"But it's not as simple as that," she warned. "The children in the pods are in induced comas at varying stages of having their imaginations drained."

"Wait, can you send me the circuit diagrams and programme code you use for the extraction?" asked Chen excitedly. "I have an idea."

"Downloading them now Chen," said Kodomo. "Be careful, Manners will stop at nothing to protect his..." the fuzzy holograph crackled and cut out abruptly.

"It looks like the kids' heads are covered in lots of electrodes," explained Chen. "If I can flick the switch controlling the imagination part (the occipital lobe in the lower back part of the brain) then I can reverse the extraction. Then if I stimulate the front part of the brain which controls motor function, they should be able to wake up and move again. I just need to get to the supercomputer."

"I can handle the guards" said Anaya.

"I know Mike Junior, I can deal with him," said Penelope firmly.

"Hello From the Other Side"

"Mike Manners is MINE," said Lil, "I have a hunch we can expose him to the world if we play our cards right."

"Are we ready? Let's go big or go home!" exclaimed Anaya, high-fiving Lil.

The train pulled into Manners Station.

CHAPTER II

PLAN B

Exiting the SSSS arrival cupboard, the gang of four entered Manners Inc., just inside a giant pair of gilded gates. A sickly sweet voice greeted them through a speaker, "Welcome to the place where Manners Magic comes to life, where dreams really do come true."

"This is giving me the creeps," said Lil. "It's just like that 'perfect' world stuff I saw in the new Oggle Goggles. Let's get on with it so we can get out of here. Chen, this is the recording I made of Kodomo," Lil replaced a cassette in her recorder, handing the used one to Chen.

Plan B

"Old-school, I like it," said Chen and Lil blushed.

Once inside Manners Towers, they saw the doors to the secret facility, at the end of a corridor, criss-crossed with laser security beams.

"Anaya, take Pen and Lil via the alternative route to avoid the motion sensors, and I'll just convert this cassette tape to digital and trick the system into thinking I'm Kodomo," said Chen.

Rigged up with harnesses and suction cups on their hands and feet, Anaya led Pen and Lil up the wall and across the ceiling.

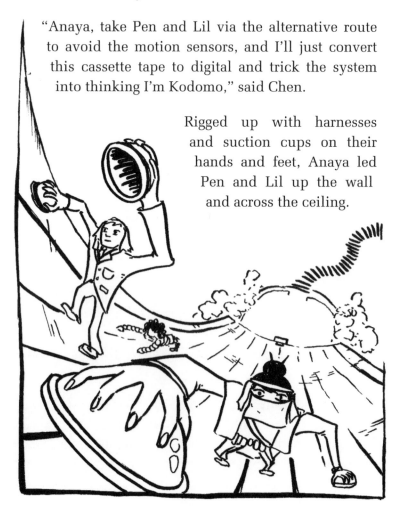

Chapter 11

Lil crawled slowly, desperate to reach the end but worried that if she went too fast she'd break more than one vacuum seal at a time and crash down onto the hard floor, activating the alarm system, with who knew what terrible consequences.

"You'd better hurry Chen. My spidey skills are more on the squished side right now," pleaded Lil.

"Perfect world," they heard the voice of Kodomo say, and the giant doors at the end of the corridor flew open as the laser beams de-activated. They'd made it.

Just inside stood Kodomo herself. She handed Chen, Penelope and Lil white M-logo'd lab coats and i.d. badges.

"Here goes nothing," said Penelope. Taking a deep breath she marched towards the billionaire's son, MJ, who was seated at his supercomputer, engrossed in his Pineapple Phone GX.

Anaya darted unseen like a squirrel up to Manners' glass skybox whilst Lil just stared in horror at the thousands and thousands of pods housing children of all shapes and sizes, looking for Toby.

"Hello Master Manners. My name is Penelope. You may remember me from that rather dull state banquet last week. Or perhaps not, as you seemed to be more interested in your Pineapple Phone… Anyway, I digress, I am here on behalf of my father, Sir Digby Davenport, to do an urgent, random, health and safety check, pre-agreed with your father, Mr Manners. Be a good chap and step away from your desk so my colleague can examine the supercomputer."

"We were expecting this, MJ, best let them get on with it," Kodomo smiled her approval.

Manners Junior – completely mesmerised by Penelope's extremely proper English and used to never questioning what he was told – obeyed immediately.

He stood up next to her, transfixed, until Penelope asked:

"Would you mind popping off and fetching us all a cup of tea? I'm simply gasping." Mike Junior jogged obediently off to the kitchenette.

Kodomo pointed discreetly to show Lil where Toby's pod was. Lil looked down at her sleeping brother's face, terrified he might never wake up.

Chen worked quickly at the supercomputer, punching keys and flicking switches.

Grunts and heavy thumping noises came from above as Anaya tackled the security guards.

All was going to plan.

Suddenly, Chen froze. He signalled to Penelope and Lil and whispered, "There's a glitch. The feed re-introducing the kids' imaginations into the occipital lobe is instead going into the medial temporal lobe."

"What does that mean, exactly?" whispered Lil urgently.

"It means their imagined thoughts and dreams are replacing the actual memories of their real lives. They are going to wake up with even less of an idea of what's real then they had before the extraction," said Chen.

Lil gasped, "Toby will believe he's a cross between an intergalactic samurai and Lionel Messi, living in a Skate Park Manga Universe! We can't let that happen. I want the original Toby back, even if he is stubborn, annoying, lazy and giving me a heart attack right now..."

"I don't know if I can do it," said Chen.

"You can do this, you are Chen, the great computer scientist and elite member of the CWLC," urged Lil.

Chen breathed deeply and concentrated hard. He began to mutter as

Plan B

his hands flew over the keyboard in a blur, "stop waking up... block stimulation of front of brains... cancel deletion of memories... put imaginings and dreams back... switch feed from centre of brain to lower back of brain."

Chen pounded the air in triumph and grinned. "I did it. Five more minutes and these kids wouldn't have remembered a thing, but now they should be returning back to normal."

Wh... wh... wh-what have you done?" Mike Junior had returned, with a tray of tea for Penelope. As he looked around he could see pods starting to open.

"And I even brought you doughnut holes with sprinkles to go with your tea. How could you? You've woken them all up! They're meant to be asleep!"

"No, Manners Junior, they're meant to be awake," replied Penelope tersely. "They are living breathing children, they're not meant to be lying in pods linked up to your machine."

"Daaaaddddd!" MJ stormed off, bounding up the stairs to his father's office.

Lil rushed to Toby's side.

Around them thousands of children were yawning and stretching as they came round.

Chapter 11

"When you are fully awake, Toby Brown, you are going to get a piece of my mind…"

"What's going on?" asked Toby, sitting up. "I've had the strangest dream where Ronaldo is dressed in dark flowing robes, on a skate board and tells Messi he is his father. It's going to make the best football video game ever… Do I start my job now?"

"You muppet," answered Lil, giving her brother a big squeeze. She decided to leave the lecture for now, seeing as he had almost had his brain drained.

CHAPTER 12

WHO RUNS THE WORLD?

Anaya reappeared, pulling with her a reluctant Mike Manners and a pale looking MJ by his side. Behind them were Sir Digby Davenport, President Ping and King Phat.

"Dad! What are you doing here?" chorused Pen, Chen and Anaya.

"We were here for the World Leaders Book Club," said Sir Digby. "Mike is our most recent member."

"You allowed Mike Manners into your book club?" asked Pen incredulously.

"Well he does run his own island, so strictly speaking, he is one of us," replied Sir Digby.

"We did become suspicious when all he wanted to read was 'The Matrix', Sun Tzu's 'The Art of War' and Marvel and Manga comics," said King Phat.

"And the level of offence he took to my suggestion of reading 'Malala' was quite extraordinary!!!" Sir Digby chimed in.

"We really knew something was up when he suggested we change our laws to make schooling optional," added President Ping. "That's why we all decided to put Kodomo undercover within his operation."

"I want a word with you," declared Lil, turning to Mike Manners and switching on her recording device. "Help me understand, how does a rich, brilliant man like you end up luring children away under false pretences?"

Who Runs the World?

It was clear that it had been a very long time since anyone had stood up to Mike Manners. He went bright red and started wagging his finger in Lil's face, yelling, "What do you know about it, you're just a child! If you'd been brought up properly like my boy MJ, you'd do as you're told and everyone would be happy.

"MJ, you know what to do now, don't you son?" Mike Manners motioned to his son.

"Yes Dad," nodded MJ. He slunk unnoticed back to his supercomputer as his father continued to rant at the gathering.

"I know what's best for everyone, no one can run things as well I can!" Manners continued. "I mean it's obviously true, I'm the most successful businessman in the world with the best products and the best ideas".

Lil stood her ground. "What about this so-called 'perfect' world you're creating for people to live in through their Oggle Goggles? Who gave you the right to decide how the world, and our experience of it, should be?"

Mike Manners snapped back, "I don't make people buy Oggle Goggles. People have a choice. People love them. They love being in Manners World, it's perfect, it's the best world ever. What's not to love?"

"But your 'perfect world' comes at the price of thousands of children's lives," accused Lil passionately. "You're

not just taking them away from their families, from their friends, from the real world, but also from getting an education."

"Kids shouldn't be forced to go to school!" shouted Mike Manners. "I'm protecting these children. School is a horrible place with monsters who bully you and make you feel small!"

Mike Manners started to sniff.

Who Runs the World?

The world leaders looked away uncomfortably.

"I'm a good person. I just want to make the world a perfect place – where everyone looks the same and behaves the same way, where everyone understands each other perfectly and everything is safe, clean, and beautiful. You can tell I'm a good guy. I donate to charidy – did you know I even donate a dollar to Save the Cute Puppy for every pair of Oggle Goggles sold."

"No amount of cute puppies can make up for what you've done," Lil said fiercely. She switched off her recorder and passed it back to Chen.

"Chen, please send this recording out to global news outlets so everyone can hear what's really been going on at Manners, Inc. and the sinister truth behind Manners World."

Slowly Toby was getting the gist of what had been happening. He'd been duped into nearly having his brain drained, and worst of all he wasn't getting his dream job. This Tuesday had turned out a lot less like winning the cup final and more like sitting SATs on your birthday.

CHAPTER 13

THE WRITING'S ON THE WALL

The world leaders were exchanging nervous glances.

"Look Mike," began King Phat, "it's been really great working with you and everything and I really like the M-Shades you sent for me, but this is all a bit embarrassing you see. I mean, we all feel a bit differently than you do about children. Mine are the future of my country and I want to educate them all to make happy, healthy citizens who will worship and respect me and my family for generations to come."

"And the thing is," continued President Ping, "we need to educate our children as much as possible so they can build fair and better futures for us all. I mean I don't necessarily want them disagreeing per se, with me or the Party but they do need skills and knowledge for our country to continue to be a success."

"Well we certainly won't be any part of this," interrupted Sir Digby Davenport, "and our children definitely won't. I'm not having that sort of thing

The Writing's on the Wall

going on, Penelope would never forgive me. While I do believe I know best, as my Penny keeps reminding me, the people need to be allowed to choose their own way, and a good all-round education is the best way to give them that choice".

"And to think," he added indignantly, looking at the other world leaders, "we invited him to join the book club! We really must review our entry policies."

"Now let's get these children back home!" Penelope was all business, as she efficiently arranged transfers for them all on the SSSS. "I'm afraid it will be worse than the London Underground in rush hour, but that's the last of them and they'll all be back safely within the next few hours."

Suddenly, the lights in the building flickered and the room went dark and silent for a moment, just King Phat's bejewelled epaulets twinkling in the gloom. A mist of dry ice rose up around the gathering.

"What now?" asked Toby, thinking how good tea and toast in front of the tv would taste right now.

"It's some kind of power surge," said Chen.

The lights came back up and no-one could quite believe their eyes. The thousands of pods and all the complex equipment, electrodes and tubes had completely disappeared. All that remained was an empty space - a gigantic expanse of shiny white warehouse.

"What...?"

"How...?"

Mike Manners was shaking with laughter. "That's my boy, MJ."

❀ ❀ ❀ ❀

Toby turned the volume up on the tv in the kitchen back home.

"...Totally fake. That recording of me, admitting to stealing children's imaginations, is totally fake news." Mike Manners was talking animatedly at a group of gathered reporters. "I never said those things. Where is the evidence for these accusations? World leaders are simply jealous of my success. Now who would like their free pair of Oggle Goggles? Come on down to Manners Tower – for a limited time only, my son and I will be handing them out in person!"

Toby and Lil sat staring at the screen, mugs of tea mid-sip.

Was Mike Manners really going to get away with it?

THE END

(OR IS IT?)

ACTIVITIES

PENELOPE AND SIR DIGBY DAVENPORT

- Why is Penelope so proud of her system of government?

- Is she right to be?

- What are the pros and cons of a government getting elected every 4 years?

- What do you think are the pros and cons of a popular vote?

- Why do you think just over half of the people who are allowed to vote, do vote?

- Do you think you should be able to vote before you are 18?

Activities

Imagine you are the leader of the Orange team in the upcoming election. What promises are you making? Design a poster to promote yourself.

CHEN AND PRESIDENT PING

- Can you think of 3 or more reasons why people might like or dislike a one-party state?

- Can you think of any checks to the power of the party?

- What are the pros and cons of a strict school system?

- Why do you think China introduced a one child policy? What are the benefits? What issues might there be?

Activities

If everyone had to wear the same outfit and have the same haircut how would you make it look?

ANAYA AND KING PHAT

- Why do you think he wears such a fancy outfit?

- Even though he is the supreme ruler, do you think there are any checks to his power?

- Why do you think some people do not want to see change (eg. Educating girls)?

- Where else in with world do girls not have access to full-time education?

- When did girls start receiving full-time education in your country?

Activities

Design a new outfit for King Phat. Remember, he wants to stand out and look phabu-lous.

Activities

MJ AND MIKE MANNERS

- What is the appeal of Manners Inc. to Toby? Does it appeal to you? Why?

- Why do you think Mike Manners has been able to gain the power he has? Why is he the boss?

- If Toby loses his memory will he still be Toby? Think about what makes a person who they are

- What are the pros and cons of the creation of virtual worlds?

Activities

Design the latest gadget for Manners Inc. Could it save the world?

UTOPIAS

- What's your idea of a perfect society. How would you organise it? Who would make the rules? Draw it and describe it here

ANSWERS

Send your answers to us at info@rapscallionpress.com for the chance to win a trip to Manners World (just kidding), but we do love hearing from our readers.